MR. BUMP

by Roger Hargreaves

EGMON

This is the sad story of Mr Bump.

The trouble was that Mr Bump just could not help having little accidents.

If there was something for Mr Bump to bump into, he'd bump into it all right.

For instance.

If you were to see Mr Bump out walking down a street in your town, and if there happened to be something to bump into down that street, then you know what would happen, don't you?

BUMP!

Mr Bump was just the same at home.

He lived in an extremely nice home, but even there he couldn't help having those little accidents.

For instance.

One morning, when Mr Bump went outside his house, he noticed that the chimney pot had come loose in a storm the night before.

"I must fix that before it falls off," thought Mr Bump to himself, and he hurried to his garden shed to fetch a ladder.

It was a very long ladder!

Mr Bump walked up the garden path with the ladder on his shoulder. He turned the corner of the garden path.

CRASH! went the living room window.

"Oh dear," thought Mr Bump, and he turned to see what had happened.

CRASH! went the kitchen window behind him.

"Oh dear," thought Mr Bump again, and he rested the ladder against the wall of the house so that he could climb up on to the roof to mend the chimney pot.

CRASH! went the bedroom window!

So you can see how Mr Bump had his little accidents!

Mr Bump had had many jobs, but somehow they never seemed to last very long.

As soon as anything got lost or broken or splintered or chipped or snapped or cracked or torn or burst or wrenched or crunched or split or slit, Mr Bump got the blame.

For instance.

When Mr Bump worked on a farm, he tripped over the farm dog and spilt the milk which he was carrying for the farmer's wife, and which the farm cat lapped up.

For instance.

When Mr Bump was a postman, he got his hand stuck in a pillar box, and they had to fetch the fire brigade to come and set him free.

For instance.

When Mr Bump was a bus conductor, he fell off the bus and couldn't catch it up again, and all the passengers travelled without having to pay.

BUS STOP

For instance.

When Mr Bump was a carpenter, he found that when he was hammering nails he hammered his thumb most of the time and the nail hardly at all.

In order to recover from this series of rather unfortunate happenings, Mr Bump decided to take a holiday. There he could think about what sort of job he could do where he wouldn't be such a nuisance to everybody.

So off he set to the station to catch a train to the seaside.

While Mr Bump was on holiday, several things happened.

For instance.

He fell off a boat into the sea and the lifeboat had to come and rescue him.

For instance.

One day, when he was quietly walking along the beach minding his own business, he got his foot stuck in a bucket, and as he couldn't get it off he had to walk around with it on his foot for hours.

For instance.

Another time he was walking along the beach, when he walked straight into a large hole that somebody had dug, and he had to stay there all night because he couldn't climb out on his own.

However, despite all these little accidents, Mr Bump enjoyed his holiday, and while he was there he had a splendid idea about what sort of job he should do.

It was quite the best idea Mr Bump had ever had. An absolutely splendid idea.

And now Mr Bump works happily for Mr Barley the farmer.

Mr Barley has a rather large apple orchard on his farm, and that's where Mr Bump works.

Mr Bump's job is picking apples. But he doesn't use a ladder to climb up the tree to pick the apples like other apple pickers.

Oh no. Mr Bump has a much better way of picking apples than that!

He just walks about!

And before long Mr Bump, being Mr Bump, walks into a tree.

BUMP!

And down falls an apple. And Mr Bump catches it.

This makes the job of apple picking much easier, and Mr Bump is very pleased about his new job, and Mr Barley is very pleased about his new apple picker.

So you see, the story of Mr Bump isn't such a sad story after all. And if you ever bump yourself, you know what to do, don't you?

Go and eat an apple picked by Mr Bump, and then you won't feel your bump at all.

You'll remember that the next time you have a bump, won't you?

Good!